ARTIVERSE PUBLICATION
PRESENTS

My Epiphany

Author
Dr. G. Youveniya

ARTIVERSEPUBLICATION
Title: **My Epiphany**

Compiler**: Dr. G. Youveniya**
Language: **English**
Manuscript By: **Artiverse**
Edited By: **Artiverse**

ISBN **- 978-81-997479-3-7**
Price: **299/-**

Distributed By: Amazon, Kindle, Flipkart, Meesho, Google Play Books and offline bookstores

Published by **ARTIVERSE PUBLICATION**
Prakhar Agrawal
MIG – 83, Bandhavgarh Colony, Satna, Madhya Pradesh, Pin Code - 485005

Email id: **artiverse81@gmail.com**
Mobile no: **9179591620**

Preface

The journey toward inner clarity often begins in the quiet spaces of the soul, where the clamour of the world fades into a whisper of divine resonance. *My Epiphany is* a collection of quotes that serves as both a personal testament and a universal invitation to rediscover the "quiet truths" that anchor a life of purpose. Drawing from over seventeen years of experience as an educator and a life rooted in the dual pillars of Faith and Love, Dr. G. Youveniya explores the intricate architecture of human emotion, from the "muscular bond" of companionship to the profound surrender of one's will to the Holy One. This collection does not merely observe life; it interrogates the nature of freedom, the dichotomy of money and morals, and the transformative power of grace, which flows "like dawn spilling gold across the sky". Through these poems, readers are encouraged to navigate their own "inward and outward" journeys, moving away from the muzzles of ignorance toward a life of integration, sanctification, and boundless mercy. It is an offering of peace and humility, crafted for those who seek to find their own "marker" in the vast realm of eternity.

Disclaimer

The poetic reflections contained within *My Epiphany* represent the deeply personal, spiritual, and philosophical journey of Dr. G. Youveniya. While these verses explore universal themes of faith, morality, and the human condition, they are a heartfelt expression of the author's individual convictions and her devotion to a life guided by humility and grace. Readers are invited to engage with these works as a subjective exploration of inner clarity and quiet truths rather than as a definitive theological or sociological treatise. The interpretations of "truth," "freedom," and "morality" presented herein are reflective of the author's prismatic view of life and her specific spiritual path. Consequently, the publisher and author provide these poems for contemplative and aesthetic purposes, acknowledging that the spiritual experiences and internal realizations described are unique to the author's own "awakening" and may resonate differently with each individual reader.

About the Publication

Welcome to Artiverse Publications — a home where creativity is not measured, ranked, or raced, but respected, nurtured, and celebrated.
Artiverse is more than a publication; it is a metaverse for artists, built by art-lovers who believe that creation deserves empathy, encouragement, and a platform that truly understands its value.

At Artiverse, we do not believe in pitting artists against one another. Our purpose is to uplift, support, and honour every creator's journey. Whether you are an intern learning the craft, a writer finding their voice, an artist experimenting with styles, or a performer expressing through sound—
You are family to us.

To support diverse artistic expressions, Artiverse Publications stands on three strong creative pillars, each playing a vital role in shaping our community
Our aim is to polish writing skills, encourage growth, exchange learning, and build a genuinely accessible literary space for writers across the globe. While we often guide and teach, we believe learning is mutual—many times, we grow through our writers too.

The Word Bond directly connects with Artiverse Publications, as exceptional writers are approached to lead projects, anthologies, and official publications.

It is an open, accessible platform where artists can share, showcase, and shine without fear of judgment. As Artiverse Publications expands, the Artisan's Asylum plays a crucial role in discovering and nurturing visual art that complements storytelling, design, and creative projects.

Further we have An Audio Club that provides a wider exposer to the storytellers, comedians and singers by organising open mics for all

At the core stands Artiverse Publications—the powerhouse that transforms art into opportunity.
It serves as a gateway for creators to publish and earn through their work, ensuring their art reaches readers beyond geographical boundaries. Selected works are officially published on platforms such as Amazon, Flipkart, and Kindle, giving artists the recognition and reach they deserve.

Now that you have a clearer picture of Artiverse as a publication-driven creative metaverse, we are grateful to have you with us. This space will grow stronger, richer, and more meaningful with your creativity, trust, and love.

First Edition

Published independently by Artiverse

Acknowledgement

It is my immense pleasure to express my heartfelt gratitude to everyone who supported the creation of this collection. I am deeply grateful to Prakhar (Dev) Agrawal, Founder of Artiverse Publication, and the entire Artiverse team for their expert guidance, professionalism, and encouragement throughout this journey. My sincerest thanks go to my parents, my husband, and my son for being my greatest strength, and to my friends for their unwavering belief in me. Finally, I thank you, the reader, for giving these poems purpose; it is my hope that these verses offer you meaningful moments of reflection and resonate deeply within your heart.
Thank you.

Regard,
Dr. Youveniya

About the Book

In My Epiphany, she records the epiphany moments that illuminate life's journey — moments of clarity that inspire simplicity, humility, and inner strength. Her words are not merely quotations, but distilled reflections born of lived experience and deep contemplation. Through this collection, Dr. Youveniya invites readers to pause, reflect, and awaken to the quiet truths that shape a meaningful life.

About the Founder

He is an emerging writer, motivated by a thoughtful desire to provide healing and support to as many people as possible. His supreme happiness comes from seeing the smiles on the faces of people, he touches with his words, and he's dedicated to inspiring and motivating people in his community to achieve their dreams. He determinedly believes in the power of spreading positivity far and wide. His quotes, stories, and poems draw inspiration from both the real-life experiences of others and the limitless realms of his imagination.

IG - words.bydev

Call - 9179591620

Mail – devkumar120803@gmail.com

About the Author

Dr. G. Youveniya

Dr. G. Youveniya is a devoted teacher and reflective writer with more than 17 years of experience in education. Her life and work are guided by the twin investments of Faith and Love, which she believes are the true wealth of human existence.

Life’s crux is in living the very moment.

Your ‘Words’ determine your ‘World’.

Mercy: the magnanimous magnitude of ‘forgiveness’.

“Love”is the only trajectory, present by Christ, to an empyrean living.

Betrayal of a friend is the cruelest of all vices.

Imagination is the catalyst for creativity.

Life is all about being prepared for God's will rather than planning to one's own will.

College: the production unit of our nation's future architects.

Every past memory has to be
recycled for a better future.

Prayer is the grandeur luxury of communion with God.

Worship is the highest expression of awe and wonder of God's Grandeur.

Clarity amidst confusion;
calmness amidst chaos; is the
confirmation of communion with
CHIRST.

As a raindrop is transformed into
a pearl inside the oyster; so, will a
man be transformed in the
wounded hands of the savior.

Nature: the breathtaking awe of
God's grandeur.

Maturity elevates the altitude of thinking.

As a pencil without its lead; a pen without the ink, is useless, so is man without morals.

With every form of light its heat is also felt.

Green and blue, will become a rare hue, amidst the lifeless field of skyscrapers.

The silent valley in its silence speaks volumes of human's simpleness.

Chance is life's unpredictable moment.

Breath is the product of lungs
(rented air) until the stillness
props in.

Monotony curbs creativity.

I love the ‘lover of my heart’.

‘Love’ harmonizes two hearts;
‘Marriage’ approves the harmony,
and the ‘Harmony’ends in
‘Eternity’.

Sex is the fusion of two souls into one; both in mind and body.

Your ‘Wait’ is the testimony of your ‘Faith’.

‘Faith’ frees everyone from the world’s estrangements.

Reflections: the recollection of detailed imprints of an observation.

Life is solitary travel towards solitudinous solace.

With God, life is a bliss.

Procrastination is the willing suspension of discipline.

Sun: the eraser of darkness.

Emotions make life colourful.

A leader is a visionary with an elevated perspective.

Learning is a lifelong luxury.

Cross: the authentic symbol of love and redemption.

Discipline makes you the discipline of success.

Food: the imprisoner of all senses.

Fear besieges both reason and logic.

Sea: the reflection of heaven above.

Growth is also wild unless pruned.

Flowers bloom in obedience to the creator not to his creations, so are we in life be bloomed.

Life is an exhilarating exploration
of uncertainties with certainty.

Prayer is not a part of life but the act of life.

Beauty, entices the beholder.

Childhood, the envisage of all virtues.

Time, the colossal entity of eternity.

As the night awaits the dawn, so do we await the second coming of the light – Jesus Christ.

Life at large, is a miniscule in God's time.

Love should be shown on demand
only as to be prevented from
being vulnerable.

Debt prorogates any relationship.

Rain: God's abstergent gift
nature.

Life is a conglomeration of
choices, either of forte or foible.

Education is the path to self-exploration.

Humbleness: the state of total self-surrender to the supreme power.

Love harmonizes two hearts,
marriage approves the harmony
and the marriage ends in eternity.

Prayer, the purgatory of human soul.

‘Reason’ and ‘Logic’ are the weeds that grow in the garden of ‘Faith’.

Life becomes worthy, when aligned to God's plan only.

The irony of life: all that are priced are valuable; all that are priceless are invaluable, yet life is forfeited to the valuable rather the invaluable.

Grave: the unsolicited second womb of a human.

GOD, the manifestation of truth, light and love.

"Empathy" is the rarest jewel that adorns the heart.

Education is the illuminating light that eradicates the ignorance of night.

Life is a pilgrimage towards eternity.

Luxury is in the state of mind rather than the possession of things.

Life is permeated with potential possibility to explore new horizons.

Language: the laconic lustre of human expression.

Communication is to union for a cation.

Time transcends one’s journey towards maturity.

Expect the impossible to have it possible in life.

To start a year is a gift; to finish it is a blessing.

Marriage: God's crafting of two soul, mind, and life in his branch.

Faith determines the future.

Revision: realigning our vision with God's.

Sanctification is the Divine's cleansing.

Self-denial : The willingness to forage one's will.

Imagination is the mind's agility
to visualize the unseen beliefs.

Imagination is the mind's agility
to visualize the unseen beliefs.

Manifestation: The innate magnetic power to attract Divine's will on oneself.

Sacrifice: The willingness to nullify one's priority over others.

Salvation: The unexpected invitation to glory, though being unworthy.

Grace: Divine's love on human race.

Discipline: The voluntary embracement of repetitive work aligned with time

Disobedience: The state when human pride entrenches itself against obedience.

Self-indulgence stagnates spiritual growth.

Salvation is the remission of one's sins.

Service : The exponential expression of goodwill.

Devotion: The overflow of superabounding sense of gratitude.

Discipleship: One's rightful acceptance to surrender oneself to the other.

Proclamation: To claim one's faith in God.

Repentance: The confession of guilt that separates one from God.

Encroachment: The thoughts that hinder Divine's intervention.

Obstinacy: The blind belief in the Self.

Conviction: The sure affirmation in one's belief.

Determination is the alchemy that transmutes trials into triumphs.

Chasterning is the expression of
Love's sternness.

Redemption redefines the past to reshape the future.

Redemption is Divine's rewritten life.

www.ingramcontent.com/pod-product-compliance
Lightning Source LLC
Chambersburg PA
CBHW062143160726
48282CB00027B/923
* 9 7 8 8 1 9 9 7 4 7 9 3 7 *